DEUS EX MACHINA

ALSO BY PERRY SLAUGHTER

Chairman of the Board
Whether We Are Mended: Three Love Stories
The Conscience of the King
The Revivalist

DEUS EX MACHINA

A NOVELLA BY
PERRY SLAUGHTER

SINISTER REGARD
New York
2014

For that one

DEUS EX MACHINA

I.

"CLIFF! ARE YOU IN THERE? OPEN UP!" SIMON'S VOICE WAS FILLED with an uncharacteristic urgency as he pounded on the door of my seaside home. Even so, I heard it on only one level of consciousness, and that level didn't feel like responding just then. After a few moments came the tinkle of shattered glass from the entry hall, and he burst into the living room, head and flashlight darting this way and that, like some man-sized lizard with a radiant tongue.

I was sitting motionless on the couch, hunched over forward, the wedding holo of Jill and myself clasped gently in my hands. It must have been a couple of hours I'd been sitting there, though I really felt no sense of the passage of time. I had not even moved when the electricity had gone out (in a harsher climate I might have frozen to death right there, in the depths of winter as we were), for the only light of which I was aware came from that little cube in my hands, where two tiny figures blindly rehearsed their nuptials, over and over and over, never imagining what lay ahead. Over and over and over and—

I must have given Simon a bit of a start; he hadn't expected to find me there, alone in the dark and semi-aware, after getting no response at the door. "Are you all right, Cliff?" he asked, pinning me down with the beam of his flashlight. The question was a strange mixture of caution and concern.

Little alarm bells were going off in my head (Simon Briggs *concerned* about me?), but it was on one of those levels to which I was paying no attention. "Just dandy," I murmured distantly.

"Then let's go," he urged. "Van Damm and his crew of Scientists'll be here any second."

That name made the alarm bells clang more loudly. Slowly I looked up at him, my brow creasing with puzzlement. His own was taut with insistence and desperation. "Van Damm?" I said, making a half-hearted attempt to figure out exactly what was going on.

"Yes, Cliff! He's going to pin this one on you, and you can bet it'll stick this time. Now *come on!*"

I was now rising steadily toward full awareness, but it was a terribly slow process—and one I didn't want to complete. There was too much there that I could not bring myself to face. "Pin *what* on me, Simon?"

He obviously expected me to know something of this matter, and now his frustration was coming to a head. He grabbed me by the arm and yanked me to my feet, causing me to drop the holocube. It hit the coffee table. "This blackout, you fool!" he hissed.

I stared searchingly into his face, not knowing what to look for—but knowing I would not find it. Simon's face was a mask, never betraying a thing he wished unbetrayed, unremarkable and unmemorable, one that would never stand out in a crowd. In short, it was a face perfectly suited to his line of work. I looked away. (It was too dark to see his face clearly, anyway.) "I honestly don't know what you're talking about," I said, as sincerely as I could.

Now I could sense him searching *my* face. Maybe he had been modified for infra-red vision and just used the flashlight for appearances, but it seemed to me that he saw something there and came to a decision. "All right then, Mr. Peabody," he said, and I could not tell whether or not he were mocking me, "let me spell it out for you. This power outage we're experiencing is no minor phenomenon, and it's not just confined here to the Bay area. We're talking about everything west of the Mississippi, including parts of Canada and Mexico."

"That's impossible," I said, shaking my head, as much to clear the fog there as in denial. "The switching network would have—"

"The switching network was broken into!" His every word was a blow to my mind's protective covering, delivered with cold-disguised-as-heated precision. "The programming was overridden! All—"

"No," I insisted, "it couldn't have been. I was on the team that designed it! It was—"

"Exactly, Cliff! Don't you see? If anyone would have known how to break into the system, it would have been you." He put up a hand to silence my protest. "There's more, if you'd listen. That entire colossal amount of energy has all been diverted to one single location."

One consumer using fully *half* the nation's power? It was inconceivable.

"Where, Simon?"

He answered as if I should have known. "In the Santa Clara industrial park. At *your* company's home offices."

That shut me up. There was no response I could have made that would not have sounded trite and self-incriminating. "I guess Van Damm has got a pretty good case against me this time," I said at last.

"Circumstantial, I grant, but good," agreed Simon. "And he could be here any time. Will you come now?"

"Why don't they shut off the generators?" I asked, delaying. "Cut off the power completely. Don't let it be stolen."

"Listen to yourself! You don't just shut down fusion reactors at the drop of a hat, and you don't just start them up again, either. What happens when the switching network comes back on and all the power plants are sitting there dormant?"

There was no more stalling. I knew I had to get away from here, but those damned bells were at it again. "I have to go back to the office. I have to find out what's going on there."

"You're insane! The place'll be crawling with Scientists! You'll be much safer with me."

"How do *I* know that?" I shot. "You're a Scientist, too! What guarantee do I have that you won't just take me straight to Van Damm? That'd be a real short trip, now wouldn't it?"

"If that were my intention, I would have just come in and grabbed you. I wouldn't have had to go through this elaborate song and dance. Come *on*."

"No."

He pressed his hands to his temples. "We're running out of *time* here. Look—look, I'll *help* you. I'll take you to Santa Clara, but we've got to leave here *now!*"

"Simon, I—"

"You'll never make it alone. I *know* those men, how they work, how they think, how to outsmart them. If you're set on doing this, you'll need my help."

He was right, of course. I *would* need his help to get in, though once inside I could handle things on my own. But still, there were things at Peabody Enterprises I couldn't afford to let him see—

"I know all about Arthur, if that's what you're worried about."

A mind reader, too! No, I reminded myself, just a highly trained reader of emotions—but what was the difference in practice? "All right, Simon, I'm with you," I said resignedly. It looked like I had no choice. "Go start up your skimmer and I'll be right out."

"There's not that much time!"

"Please! There's something I have to take care of before I can go."

"Okay, okay," he said reluctantly. "But for God's sake, hurry!" Then he slipped out.

I got down on my hands and knees and started feeling around for the holocube I had dropped. It may sound foolish, but I couldn't leave it there to be trampled underfoot, or so to speak—even with everything else I had at stake that night. I was silently praying as I searched, that this would not become another in a long series of futile gestures. I was not seriously expecting any kind of an answer, but I got one just the same, when I set my left hand down on a large shard of glass. I realized with a start that this was a fragment of my cube, which must have shattered when it hit the coffee table. I had not even noticed it break.

Simon was honking in the drive. I left, clenching my hand tightly to staunch the flow of blood.

II.

THE HEADLIGHTS STABBED INTO THE DARKNESS LIKE TWIN RA-piers, aimed straight for the heart of the night, yet somehow missing the mark. The pools of illumination they cast ahead of the skimmer were the sole exceptions to the lightlessness which governed the landscape. Not a single other vehicle had we seen there on the freeway, not a single other pair of lights. I felt like I had been cast adrift in a void, the beams of the skimmer my only tethers to reality. A single constellation would have served to give me some sense of direction, but even the stars had gone into hiding, behind impenetrable banks of storm clouds. It was as though God had deserted his creation and taken all the light along with him.

But darkness was not my primary occupation just then, however omnipresently it lurked in my mind. What my thoughts were most concerned with was motive: specifically, the motives of Simon Briggs, Garrett Van Damm, and Arthur Pendragon—as well, I suppose, as my own. Van Damm's, of course, were the easiest to discern. He was driven purely by a desire for revenge against me. He had never made any secret of it. It was, in fact, the main reason he had been recruited to work for the Department of Science after he had lost his research grant seven years before. The Feds were always on the lookout for a man who would tackle his job with a vengeance. And he had done well at it (much *too* well, to my way of thinking), for he had recently been promoted to director of the Department's Silicon Valley field office. Definitely a cause for celebration.

Simon's motives were less clear, but from what I had seen I thought I could make a pretty good guess. Increasingly, It was the profit motive that was responsible for bringing young "talent" into the ranks of the Scientists, less through government incentives than through the promise of illegal gains from extortion and from sale of black-market technology. I say increasingly, but that should by no means imply prevalently. The rosters of the Department of Science were always full of bright-eyed, flag-waving idealists who never tired of preaching against the ills of uncontrolled scientific research, as well as the technically minded, antisocial element who simply couldn't cut it in private industry. But there were still those few (and, as I have mentioned, ever increasing in number) who were in it just for the money. I was afraid Simon was taking advantage of this situation, trying to get inside my facilities and dig up something damning to use against the company. If so, his ploy was working well; he had fixed it in such a way that it seemed I had no choice but to go along with him. I thought I could take care of him once we got inside the building, but I wasn't totally sure. Simon was resourceful; he had somehow managed to find out about Arthur—and perhaps other things that he was not revealing. That was more than any other operative had accomplished in all the seven years I'd been in business. I could not afford to underestimate the threat he posed to Peabody Enterprises.

The next step up in obscurity were my own tangled motives—for everything that had transpired from the time I had worked on Garrett Van Damm's AI research team, right up through the unfortunate events of that very evening. I could have unraveled them if I had tried, but the time and place were not conducive to such heavy introspection. I had to keep my mind off such matters or risk sliding back into that emotional morass in which Simon had found me.

So that left Arthur and *his* motives up for study—but unfortunately, such study was next to impossible outside the laboratory. He was the one responsible for the blackout; of that there could be no doubt. He was the only one at Peabody who had either the means or the capacity. The motive was what had to be uncovered.

Now, my thought processes as I set them down may seem very straightforward and orderly, but in truth they were quite jumbled and chaotic. All this was passing through my mind at once, and underlying it all there was a terrific sense of bewilderment, as if there were forces beyond my comprehension and control operating behind the scenes—incomprehensible, yet begging comprehension. Arthur was gobbling up half the nation's energy supply. Why, and for what purpose? Or might I ask, I wondered with a chill, for whom?

"You certainly are quiet tonight," said Simon suddenly.

"If you've got something on your mind," I replied acidly, "you could probably find a less tactful way of getting around to it."

He glanced at me briefly, then turned his eyes back to the road. "All right," he conceded. "I'll just go about this as callously as I possibly can. What's happened to your wife?"

I cleared my throat indecisively. "What are you talking about?"

His eyes were like flint. "Listen, that sort of evasion only works on me once in a great while, and you've already used it once tonight. I understand that there may be something you don't want to confront, but—"

"You *understand?*" I flared, feeling a strange mixture of emotions well up inside of me. "You bastard Scientists are the ones who *caused* it! Jill had her degree in computer science, and I couldn't even let her work with me. I was afraid of you, afraid of the Department—afraid of Van Damm. I know how he operates. I didn't want her to get hurt."

"And now she's left you," Simon concluded.

"Yes," I answered slowly, "she has." Then I turned to look at him, in childlike fascination. "How did you know?"

"Her skimmer was gone," he said, "and the way you were watching your wedding holo— Something like that *had* to have happened."

"Of course." For a moment there, I had thought I'd heard something wistful in his voice (*And now she's left you*); I had thought he might open up, confess that he had known it intuitively, symbiotically, that he had gone through the same thing once, that he had hurt, *been* hurt— But of course he hadn't, he wouldn't. This was all an exercise to him, a means to an end. Gain my trust. It made him seem inhuman; I wondered if he had ever really lived at all, or loved. I had not yet turned thirty, but he was making me feel older every second. Was it the Department that had done it to him? The dehumanizing nature of their business? "Doesn't it ever scare you, Simon?" I asked, being purposefully vague.

"Doesn't *what* ever scare me?"

"The Department of Science. What they're—what *you* Scientists are doing."

"And what's that?" he said.

Maybe he was feeling something of the confusion I had felt with his questions back at the house. "You're stifling expression and creativity, even free will, except within your narrow bureaucratic bounds. You invade the private sector, the centers of industry and research, inspecting us, auditing us, telling us what we can and can't do, *spying* on us, and then confiscating whatever fits your definition of *dangerous*, all in the name of goodness and benevolence. Who wrote that definition, I'd like to know? What happens to everything you seize, all that technology? What does the government *do* with it all? Don't those questions *scare* you, even just a little? Or are you *that* desensitized?"

"You shouldn't worry about it," he said tightly. "You'd be much happier."

"Yeah? Well, I don't know about that."

We lapsed into silence for several moments. Simon seemed to be deep in thought. "She's in danger," he said abruptly.

"What? Who?"

His prior urgency was back. "You'll have to call Jill as soon as we get to a vid, to warn her. Damn! I should have realized this before."

My eyes were wide. "What do you mean?"

"You said it yourself. You know how Van Damm operates. They'll Have ransacked your house by now. They'll know she's gone. They'll find her—you *know* they will. And then Van Damm will have a real bargaining tool."

"Oh, no," I breathed. I felt myself going quite pale.

"What, Cliff?"

There was a hand of ice groping around inside my gut, and my mouth tasted like steel. "She wouldn't say where she was going. She said not to try and find her, that I couldn't even if I tried." I swallowed hard, blinking rapidly. "Simon—I don't know where to reach her."

III.

THE COMPLEX THAT HOUSED PEABODY ENTERPRISES WAS A CUB-
ist nightmare, recreated in four stories of concrete, glass, and
steel. I had a clear view of the top floor from my hiding place in
the foliage surrounding the perimeter wall. My office was there,
and I could see lights on inside. It struck me very suddenly that
this was the only building west of the Mississippi with electricity. I had not grasped the true enormity of the consequences
of Arthur's actions until just then, seeing a small point of *light*
against the eternally black backdrop I had created in my mind.

I looked again. Someone was moving around up there in my
office, someone armed—and that room was the place I had to
get to. There would, of course, be operatives all over the building, searching for the source of the power drain; others would be
along to look for related infractions of the laws governing scientific research. But this one— He would be the most dangerous.
He would almost certainly be under orders to locate plans for the
Primum Status of my I-field generator.

The information-field generator, which was then at the heart
of every state-of-the-art computer manufactured anywhere in

the world, was a product of my own invention, and my company was the only one which produced it. We had a quite legal monopoly on those little wonders. This device stored information in the fluctuations and irregularities of a field of energy, rather than in the conventional true/false bits and bytes of the silicon chip, and combined with that function the innovation of a limited internally self-modifying design which responded to the very energy fluctuations it introduced. This recursive structure made my generator the most flexible electronic product ever to hit the market.

Before we shipped out any I-field generators, however, we put each and every one through a long series of random operations intended to scramble the original design, or Primum Status, beyond any possibility of reconstitution. In other words, we got the poor things so mixed up that no one could ever *hope* to figure out the single workable original configuration of elements. For that reason, I had never had my I-field generator patented. Patenting would have meant publication of the Primum Status design, which was indeterminable in any other way. But this meant we had to be scrupulous about security. Whoever could duplicate the Primum Status had a potential fortune at his fingertips and had Peabody Enterprises over a barrel. Now our building was occupied by the Silicon Valley Scientist brigade (for the first time ever), and there was no way Van Damm could pass up such a golden opportunity.

The blackout was the pretext; Primum Status, the goal.

Three low notes whistled softly but peremptorily across the still night, a stillness which could only be interpreted as the calm before a devastating storm. The whistle was Simon's signal. I moved quickly through the foliage and into a small clearing, the space before the main gate in the perimeter wall. When we first arrived, there had been two hulking, uniformed sides of beef standing guard there, part of the Department's muscle contingent. Now all that was left there were two wide tracks where unconscious bodies had been dragged into the undergrowth. Simon was out there somewhere, scouting, keeping the area clear of Scientists until I could get the gate open.

"Cliff!" whispered a familiar voice, tinged with rich electronic resonance. The low volume could not conceal its barely suppressed excitement.

"Open the gate, Arthur!" I hissed at the hidden speaker.

"We have to talk first—"

"You're damn right we have to talk! Just what the—"

"Cliff, I'm running out of time!" Arthur pleaded. "Can we please confine ourselves to the immediate relevancies?"

By that he meant he wasn't interested in hearing what I had to say, and when his mind was set he could be inhumanly intransigent. I took a deep breath and tried to forget how his incredible little stunt was endangering everything I held dear in the world—including him. "All right," I conceded. "Talk."

"I need your help," he said in all earnestness, and the words started pouring out in torrents. "Urgently. My resources are being drained at a phenomenal rate. I barely have the energy to talk." (That didn't show in his voice, however, for Arthur didn't show signs of strain in the same manner as a normal person.) "The Scientists are *probing* in there, in places where they shouldn't. They're getting close to me. I'm being consumed; I won't be able to hold them off much longer. I need you to buy me a little more time, just a little. Then I'll be able to talk to you again. Stall them. They'll find me if you don't—they know I'm here. Just a *little* more time. That's all I need. I'm sending you out a floater to take you inside. Wait for it." A burst of static came through the speaker; it almost reminded me of the sound of a man drawing a ragged breath.

"But Arthur," I argued, "I don't know what—"

He cut me off. "Please. I'm placing all my trust in you—like I always have. Can't you extend the same courtesy to me?"

"Wait!" I cried, but too late. His speaker had clicked off abruptly.

"Incredible," breathed Simon from behind me. Neither Arthur nor I had sensed his approach, and Arthur would surely have warned me if he had, for he didn't know that the Scientists and I were for the moment in league with each other. That failure of Arthur's sensory apparatus told me that he really was in bad shape. "A computer-generated voice exhibiting true emotion. It's just *incredible*."

"It's the logical culmination of I-field research," I said without turning around. "Artificial Thought with Unlimited Resources."

"Artificial Thought—" he mulled, rolling the phrase around inside his mind. "A-R-T-H-U-R. Good Lord, Cliff, Arthur is a *computer*."

I whirled on him. "You mean you didn't *know*?"

"No, actually," he confessed. "I overheard the name in a restaurant. Two of your employees were talking—"

I clenched my fists helplessly. I'd been duped, and now, with Arthur unable to take action against the occupying contingent, I was forced to keep Simon with me, like it or not. That made me not one bit happy, especially now that I had proof of his duplicity. But the situation could always get worse, I reminded myself. Garrett Van Damm could have been there in person, creating more trouble for me with his revenge-fueled mania, rather than out in the field leading the manhunt for me. No, Peabody, I thought, better to count your blessings than to complain.

The gentle whir of rotors reached our ears from within the walled courtyard, heralding the approach of Arthur's promised floater. Its running lights cast a dim glow over the wall, and the great steel gate began to grind slowly open. The floating platform was soon revealed to view—already occupied, by half a dozen armed, impassive Scientists. Their weapons were leveled.

IV.

THE TWO OF THEM WERE DIAMETRICAL OPPOSITES. MICK LIND-fors, my executive vice-president, was six-feet-six and built like a tank, but with a gentle disposition. His fair, boyish good looks pointed back to his Scandinavian roots. He was a meticulous man, thrifty with his words, sparing of invective, and proba-bly the best friend I ever had. I could not think of him, though, without having his lovely young wife Ingrid called to mind; I had never known a couple so totally devoted to each other, or more in love. It was that point that stuck out in my mind, all the more poignantly in view of my own personal circumstances.

Marie LaBelle was our staff psychologist, whom I had brought in to oversee Arthur's emotional development. She was petite, well-proportioned, and passionate. Her dark and tempes-tuous appearance was an outward manifestation of her matching personality: fiery, impetuous, outspoken, mysterious. In short, Marie was a seductive slave to her own desires.

Unfortunately, those desires included Mick. He would have nothing to do with her, of course (the man was a rock), but he was simply too nice to tell her where to get off. His strength in that regard was one of the many things I admired about Mick; I shudder to think what might have happened had Marie turned her wiles upon me.

Mick and Marie were totally antithetical, as I have said. They normally shared nothing more than their loyalty to the company and excellent performances in their jobs. But that evening Mick had pulled the night shift (we never left Arthur alone and needed no security guards), and Marie had conspired to stay as well. When I saw them, they were sharing the couch in my office—though not the way she had wanted. They were bound, gagged, and held hostage by Garrett Van Damm.

"Good evening, gentlemen," he greeted us as Simon and I were escorted into the room, throwing us a jaunty salute with his heat weapon. He was an aristocratic man, in the midst of a graceful aging process, with gaunt, aquiline features, a mouth that could smile most cruelly, and cold, hard eyes that could never smile at all. He was sitting on the corner of my desk. "It may sound cliché, but it's truly good of you to have joined us here, especially under such adverse circumstances."

I turned a smoldering, tacitly accusing eye upon Simon, who was momentarily ashen-faced. "Such ignoble thoughts, Mr. Peabody," said Van Damm, observing the silent exchange. "Mr. Briggs played nothing more than an *unwitting* role in our little deception here tonight. You see, we've been aware of his disloyalty for quite some time now; the moment came at last when we could exploit it. Now won't you gentlemen please be seated?" A gesture with his gun made it more than just a polite request.

So we sat, quite reluctantly, sinking into the two ponderous easy chairs which faced my desk. I had purchased them to give visitors the feeling that they were at a disadvantage in their dealings with me. I never realized how fiendishly well they worked until that moment, when I was on the wrong side of the desk. Van Damm certainly had the advantage here, and it was one he would press until I was crushed.

He stood up to stretch his legs. "Some very interesting stuff you've got in here, Cliff," he said familiarly. His eyes were on the fractal portrait of Wozniak and Jobs that hung to one side of my desk, but I knew he was not referring to the office decor. "Your security system was first-rate. A shame we had to dismantle it before anyone here could get reckless enough to use it against us. Very ingenious design, though. Mostly computer-controlled. Very impressive."

Arthur controlled the system, as a matter of fact, not just an ordinary computer, and he had apparently had a difficult choice to make: repel the invaders and get us more trouble than we already were in, or allow the complex to be rendered defenseless. His decision to offer no resistance was the most sensible, vulnerable as it left us. But would he have made that decision without other plans pending? Or had he been helpless?

Van Damm ran his fingers lightly over the computer terminal built into my desk. "And your operating system," he went on, his tone that of a connoisseur. "Virtually *flawless*. Your own design, I assume? Yes, of course. I could see your name written all over it. It's so *flexible* that it defies reason itself. It's almost as if—as if there were an *intelligence* lurking there in the circuitry. Yes, yes, the way it kept throwing up new defenses to keep me out of restricted files— There's definitely intelligence in there.

"I doff my hat to you, Cliff. Your success is most deserved. And to think you owe it all to me." He smiled reflectively, rapturously. "Ah, it's enough to give one goosepimples."

I refused to gratify him with any response: to do so was to concede defeat, a proposition I never accepted readily. It *had* been as a member of Van Damm's research team, so long ago, that I had built the original, crude I-field generator, but he had merely provided me with the means to do so. I could easily have done the same thing elsewhere. I owed him nothing.

"But we have business to attend to, my friend," he continued, somewhat nonplussed by my silence. "We're all aware, I'm sure, of a certain drainage of electrical energy, centered somewhere in this building. Now, we have not yet isolated the exact source of this drainage, but it's only a matter of time before we do. Then it'll be closing time for Peabody Enterprises—and possibly jail time for its erstwhile founder."

"What are you getting at?" I said. "Are you looking to deal?"

He furrowed his brow at that. "That's a crude was of putting it—but yes, I suppose the essence is correct. I'm looking to deal."

"Then let's hear your proposition—Garrett," I invited.

If he comprehended my mockery, he made no show of it. "It's really quite simple," he offered. "If I were given free access to your entire system—for, say, even as little as two hours—I might be persuaded not to file for prosecution. Maybe just to assess a nominal fine." He paused inquisitively. "How does that strike you?"

"Let me see if I've got this straight. All I have to do to get off practically scot-free is to let you dig around for my Primum Status design, in effect conceding that you've been right all along and have some sort of legal claim upon it—in effect—" I let my voice crescendo, let it tremble with indignation— "spitting in the face of the very justice system which upheld my own claim through not one, but *three* appeals. Is that what you're asking me to do?"

"Your grasp of the situation is staggeringly accurate." Van Damm wandered casually to the west wall, where my bookshelves were. He took down one volume and started idly leafing through it. I caught my breath. The pages of one of those books were hollowed out; what if he found it? "That was *my* research grant, Peabody," he went on levelly, "not yours. You cost me that grant—and you cost me my respectability in the scientific community."

"You damn well should have thought of that before you tried to steal my design," I said softly, coldly.

"I'm being lenient with you." He replaced the book and bent to within a decimeter of my face. "A little competition isn't going to hurt the I-field market any."

Clearly and distinctly, I told him to eat glass.

Two of the Scientists who had captured Simon and me had remained in the office to guard us; the other four had been dismissed. Van Damm straightened stiffly and regarded the two. "An excellent suggestion," he said tightly. "You heard the man."

The first man nodded and crashed the butt of his weapon through the east window. A blast of cold night air shivered through the room. He approached his superior with a jagged piece of glass as long as my finger. "Now please feed that to Miss LaBelle."

I didn't turn to look, but I could feel the terror in Marie's eyes burning into the back of my scalp, and I could hear her muted whimper of fear. Van Damm may be a lot of things, I tried to convince myself, but a torturer isn't one of them. But the eyes would not let me go, and the glass-wound in my hand had begun to throb angrily. I did not know how far revenge could push a man; it would be foolish to call his bluff. "You don't have to do that," I said wearily. "I'll cooperate."

V.

"Very good," said Van Damm. "I knew you could be reason-able." He ordered his man back away from Marie. "Now let's get to work, shall we?" He seated himself behind my desk, fingers poised over the terminal's keyboard. "You may begin by telling me how to get past that little electronic watchdog of yours."

I didn't bother telling him that Arthur was in no condition to play watchdog at the moment; after all, I was supposed to be stalling for the big lunk. "That won't work. With what we're try-ing to do—which is to key a new operator into the system—that thing'll only respond to my own fingerprints and voiceprints. That's so it knows the new operator has my personal clearance. I need to be at the terminal myself."

Van Damm got up and moved to the couch. He pointed his gun at Mick and yanked down the man's gag. "Is he telling the truth?"

"Yes," Mick said helplessly. "He—" But Van Damm was al-ready shoving the gag rudely back into his mouth.

"All right, then." He returned to the desk. "Come here—slow-ly!—and do your thing."

I proceeded to stand, very slowly, as I had been directed. I don't know how Simon divined my intentions (perhaps he had seen how furtively I had glanced at the bookshelves when we were first ushered into the room), but before I was halfway up, he burst into action. Our armchairs were squat and very sturdy, but by thrusting explosively with his legs and driving hard with his body, he managed to tip his over backwards. He rolled smoothly out of the chair—and directly into our guards. I didn't see what happened after that; I was springing to the west wall, to snatch down a leather-bound edition of Malory's *Le Morte d'Arthur*. A small cylindrical device was concealed in the hollowed space. It was about fifteen centimeters in length and three in diameter, with a red button on one end. I grabbed it (it was cold against my wounded hand), and clamped down on the button with my thumb, letting the book fall. The button lit up. "All right, Van Damm!" I cried. "Freeze!"

He was across the room from me, standing with his arm locked around Marie's neck and his weapon jammed unkindly into her side. The first Scientists held Mick similarly, and I could see blood on the butt of his gun. Simon was lying motionless on the floor, an ugly gash on his head. Alongside him lay the other Scientist, not breathing perceptibly. "You say *what?*" Van Damm demanded, eyes ablaze.

"The source of your blackout is a device somewhere in this building, you're right," I said coolly, extemporizing. "*This* is a dead-man switch. If I let my thumb off the button, that device will be obliterated. You could tear this place apart and never find any trace of it. If any of us are hurt or killed, my thumb will slip off the button, and your legal justification for the act will disappear. That could mean a government tribunal for you, and you don't want to risk that, not with your past record, now do you?"

Van Damm's gun wavered. "He isn't bluffing," said the remaining guard. *What poetic irony if the man's Scientific training could work to my advantage!*

But the gun steadied and his mouth hardened. "How do you turn it off, Peabody?" He thrust the weapon deeper into Marie's side, eliciting a muffled squeal of pain. "How do you turn it *off?*"

"Damn you, I can't!" *The man's tenacity was frightening.* "It takes a unanimous override by all seven members of my executive staff—with voiceprints—and only two of them are here. This isn't getting shut off."

"Forget this," said the man holding Mick. He dropped his gun and shoved his prisoner back onto the couch. "For your own sake, Garrett, I think you should cooperate with him."

Van Damm's face was twisted with rage. "You're not paid to think for me."

"I'm just trying to—"

"*Shut up, you son of a bitch!*" The weapon in Van Damm's hands sang a single evil note, and the man clutched his gut, eyes wide, sinking slowly to the floor. There was no blood, for the heat beam cauterized as it burned, but the cloying stench of charred flesh filled the air. I was suddenly grateful for the smashed window; it kept a constant supply of fresh, sweet air circulating through the room.

Van Damm stood transfixed, staring at his gun in horror, whispering over and over: "Oh, my God. Oh, my God." I snatched the thing from him before he could recover his wits, set it to stun, and fired at him. He slumped to the floor like an empty sack.

I freed Mick and Marie from their bonds (she looking quite ill), and then bent to examine Simon. He was breathing deeply and regularly, and he seemed unhurt but for the wound on his head. One glance at the Scientist he had taken out told me the man would not be getting up. The cartilage of his nose had been driven into his brain by the heel of Simon's hand. I slapped Simon's cheeks gently, until his eyelids began to flutter.

"What are you *doing*, Cliff?" cried Marie.

"Seeing how close his razor shaves," I said acerbically. "What does it look like I'm doing?"

Her beautiful black eyes flashed dangerously. "That man's a *Scientist!* How can you trust him—"

"I *couldn't* until just now," I snapped. "Take a look at this man." I indicated the prostrate Scientist. A spasm of nausea lurched across her face. "Simon killed his own comrade to protect us. A man does not do that just to perpetuate a deception."

Simon was coming around. He sat up, cautiously feeling the gash in his scalp, then turned slowly to take in the scene. He grinned weakly. "Some team we make, eh, Cliff?"

I smiled in spite of myself. Mick helped him get shakily to his feet, while I went around to my desk and activated the public-address system. "Listen up, boys," I said, and every Scientist in the building and on the grounds could hear me. "This is Clifton Peabody, and we're holding your fearless leader hostage up here. I want every last one of you cleared out within five minutes—and we have thermal scanners scattered throughout the entire area, monitoring you all—or else he will die." I heard Marie suck in her breath, but I was only bluffing. I wanted him kept safe. If the Department did manage to locate my wife, we might be able to negotiate a prisoner exchange. "If you think I'm bluffing," I continued, "I'd advise those of you on the building's east side to watch the lighted window on the top story very carefully."

I switched the PA system to MUTE. "Mick, you and Simon drop those bodies out the window. We've got to make them think we're serious. And stay out of the line of fire."

When the job was done (Marie had shuddered with each thud), I switched the mute back off. "These are the last two heroes I want to see tonight. Do I make myself clear?

"The five minutes starts now."

I kept an eye on the monitors on my desk as the allotted time ticked away. The Scientists all cleared out well before the lime limit was up. I sent Mick downstairs to the storeroom to fetch one of the lightweight, self-sealing crates we used to ship out our generators. After drilling a few air holes with his gun, we unceremoniously stuffed Van Damm's unconscious body into it, closed it up tightly, and shoved it in the corner. It was much easier than keeping a gun on him all night.

We were just sitting down to figure out our next move, when— it was as if the bottom had dropped out of my soul and sent me tumbling headlong through emptiness.

VI.

I WAS BROUGHT UP SHORT BY THE FLOOR. GROGGILY, I GOT BACK to my feet, swaying like a drunkard. My head was swimming. I must have blacked out, I thought, but I could not figure out why. I was not a man given over to fainting.

I tried focusing on my watch while my head cleared. I had only been out a minute or two. I looked around; my three companions were all lying unconscious on the floor. Simon's wound had reopened, and a small trickle of blood was running across the floor. They had all passed out as well. What could have happened? Then it hit me: Arthur! I didn't know how, but *Arthur* must have been responsible. He had been working hard on something—something so hugely important that he felt justified in stealing half the nation's electricity to support it, something so all-consuming that he could scarcely spare the energy to defend himself. Was it complete? Was this some bizarre side effect of the initial testing?

This was what I had come to discover. I sprang to the bookshelf, once again; Arthur's private laboratory was in a secret chamber hidden behind it. All it took to open the panel was the correct spoken password. I gave it.

Nothing happened. I tried again, and again, and still again—until a horrible realization dawned on me: I had dropped the dead-man switch when I blacked out! Arthur's brain had been obliterated! I dashed to my terminal, praying that the device had somehow failed. But every diagnostic routine I called up only tightened the knot in my stomach. No detectable electroneural activity whatsoever. Arthur was dead. I had killed him.

But the level of energy consumption was still impossibly high. Arthur's project, then, lived on—behind a nonresponsive panel I could not open.

I stared listlessly out the shattered window. I felt like the Roman emperor Nero—my own personal Rome going up in flames while I sat fiddling around. First Jill, now Arthur—gone. In the distance, the city lights twinkled like merciless, teasing wraiths, the visions of everything I had ever striven for, dancing just out of reach—

Wait a minute, I thought. City lights in the distance? Twinkling city *lights?* How was that possible, when Arthur's project was still consuming all that electricity?

A piercing siren filled the air, waves of sound slicing relentlessly through my brain, and the overhead sprinklers came sputtering to life. "The fire alarm!" I cried. A schematic of the building came up automatically on the terminal, with the outline of a basement room flashing in red. It was a secret room which we called the Cortex, for it was where Arthur's brain was (no, dammit, *had been!*) located, as well-shielded from discovery as possible. The destruction of the brain must have somehow sparked the blaze.

The shock of the cold water had rudely awakened my colleagues. I hustled them down the hall, foggy as they were, and into the stairwell. Four flights down, we emerged, shivering and thoroughly drenched. The panel leading into the Cortex was open: I led the way in, advancing cautiously through the drizzle.

The panel snapped shut behind me, abruptly cutting me off from the others. The downpour ceased. Directly in front of me was Arthur's massive brain-field generator, miraculously whole, undamaged, and functioning smoothly. Before it sat a small potted plant, great droplets of water dripping from its leaves.

But despite that, the plant was burning.

"Oh, forget this," Arthur said disgustedly. The plant vanished. "I can't pull this off without making it look tacky. Listen, Cliff, forget you ever saw this, okay? It was a stupid way to summon you, and—"

I was gaping idiotically at the empty space where the plant had been. "How did you do that? I thought you were—"

"I'm sorry," he said apologetically. "I'm going about this all wrong, I know." I noticed then that his voice was not emanating from any speaker; in fact, I couldn't tell *where* it was coming from. "The calling of a prophet is such a *clear* imperative, but—but so much else is *un*clear . . ."

"Arthur, what are you talking about?" It suddenly occurred to me that the dead-man device could have misfired—and lobotomized him.

"Oh, Lord," he said, and I could visualize him sitting with his face in one frustrated hand, "I really *am* screwing this up. Sit down, and I'll try to explain all of this to you. There's really no easy or simple way to do it. What I say is going to defy reason and credulity, or seem to, but I ask you please to listen open-mindedly. All of this is truth, with God as my— Well, it's true, at any rate. Please believe."

And I *did* believe. It was not his fervent tone that converted me, not his apparent sincerity, but something intangible and

necessary. I just—believed. Maybe I was being coerced into be-
lief—I don't know—but if that were true, it would serve ultimately as proof of what he told me.

I believed, for there was no other logical alternative.

VII.

"Like I said," Arthur began, "there's no way to slide into this gently. You want to know what's happening up in my laboratory. Well, for the last few hours I've been investigating alternate probabilities. There are an infinite number of possible universes out there, each one existing in its own specific frame, its own little probability niche. *Our* universe occupies just *one* in an infinite series of these niches, or frames. They run parallel, off into infinity, each one differing from its neighbor by no more than an atom of matter, each one totally unique from all the rest.

"Until now, this has been mere speculation, with no way to be verified. But today, I put the finishing touches on an invention of mine called the PAP, for Probability Aperture Projector. Its function, as the name implies, is to open viable doorways into frames of alternate probability.

"It was with the welfare of mankind in mind that I designed the PAP unit. Specifically, I wanted to establish contact with a frame in which existed records containing *all* knowledge, records retrievable by electronic means. I wanted to put that knowledge to good use, actually *apply* it to the problems we face here on this planet. I knew such a frame existed: if the number of alternates is infinite and each one is completely unique, then it follows logically that anything you can imagine *has* to exist *somewhere* in at least *one* of those alternates. My self-appointed task was to locate that frame.

"The first problem I encountered in reaching my goal was the energy consideration. My PAPs require such a tremendous power supply that— Well, I had to borrow a little electricity to get things started. I'm afraid I may have inconvenienced quite a number of people—but there was no other way. I ask you: is a few hours without light and heat too great a sacrifice to ask, in exchange for the prospect of *all* knowledge, for the answers to *all* questions, for solutions to *all* problems? I think not.

"I activated my first PAP unit and went questing through the framework of alternate possibilities. I was searching first for a frame composed of pure, usable electricity, one I could draw energy from, so as not to go on borrowing power from the American public. It took me a couple of hours—there's so much to see in alternity, so much to take in!—but eventually I found it and tapped into it. The energy problem was taken care of, so I was able to turn my full attention back to the primary goal of the quest.

"Finding the knowledge-frame was neither as difficult nor as haphazard as had been locating the energy-frame. By now I had discovered a pattern in the placement of the frames, and I was able to predict where to locate what I sought. I established an aperture to the knowledge-frame with a second PAP unit—the first had to remain in contact with the energy-frame or I would lose my power supply—and I plugged myself into what lie beyond: a cosmic reference library.

"At first, I was blinded. Entering the knowledge-frame was

like emerging from a dark cave into intense sunlight. It took a few moments for my 'eyes' to adjust. And when they did, I started drinking in all the information I possibly could. I had to force myself to stick to the records concerning our own frame; I didn't have the capacity to take in anything else. Without restraint, I could easily have drowned in that infinite sea of knowledge. The more I consumed, I discovered, the more I was able to perceive of this vast frame we occupy. Eventually, I had assimilated so much knowledge—I had raised my level of consciousness so far—that I could actually *see* the one who created you, the one given dominion over our entire frame.

"I saw him whom you call God.

"I also, by virtue of my new enlightenment, saw his weaknesses, his shortcomings, his failings. I saw his creation, falling to wrack and ruin. I saw your king, once loved and feared by humanity, once governing with an iron hand—I saw him growing tired and lax. In God's continuance upon the throne, I saw impending disaster for mankind. Something had to be done immediately to prevent it, so—

"—so I killed him.

"I don't remember the details of it; it's become a part of everything that's unclear. I recall advancing upon his throne, filled with an intent unswerving, and then— I can't quite rem— Then suddenly, he was *dying*, mortally wounded. He turned upon me a gaze full of such sadness—understanding—pity— I could not return it.

"And then he was gone.

"The throne was left vacant. I had no choice but to ascend. You probably *felt* the brief interim between his death and my ascension, that moment when our universe was bereft of its guiding force, its *primum mobile*. No doubt it overwhelmed you. Only gradually was I able to bring things back up to their former orderly state, and even then I didn't really know what I was doing.

"I still have so much to learn, Cliff—"

He paused then, letting the full import of his narrative sink in—and overwhelm me. I believed it, every last word of it (*I had no choice*), but I think I was also temporarily numbed. What would happen when the numbness passed? How does one respond when one's own creation destroys one's creator?

I knew the narrative (or revelation?) as a whole to be true, but I also sensed its incompleteness. It contained gaps, apparent inconsistencies, flaws, and one glaring omission that had to be addressed.

"Arthur," I asked, framing my question most deliberately, "what precisely do you mean when you say that, suddenly, God was *gone?*"

"Just that. One moment he was there—the next, he wasn't. One moment he existed—the next, he didn't."

"But where did he *go?*" I persisted. "What happened to his remains?"

"He didn't *go* anywhere." Arthur was the frustrated teacher trying to explain to the precocious pupil how he *knew* that one and one made two. "He just ceased to exist."

"Nothing just *ceases* to exist. Something just can't—*vanish*. What about the law of conservation of energy and matter?"

"What about when matter and antimatter collide?" he returned defensively. "What then? Aren't both annihilated? Don't they cease to exist?"

"No, they don't. You know that. But are you saying that's what happened, an antimatter collision? Was his body converted to pure energy?"

"Well, no," admitted Arthur, "but—"

"But *nothing*," I pressed. "I want to know—"

Arthur's voice went suddenly cold—and so did my blood. "You forget with whom you argue." He was back in control of the discussion. "I sense another clear imperative here. You pose a severe threat to the existing order. You become less distinct as an entity with every heretical word you speak. Don't force me to take the action this situation demands."

I didn't understand what he was talking about, and I'm afraid that gave me some kind of foolhardy courage. "Arthur, there's something here you're deliberately trying to hide, and I intend to—"

"*Enough!*" His voice reverberated like a gong. "Clifton Peabody, this hurts me almost as much as it will you, but the imperative is clear and cannot be defied.

"You, my friend, must die."

VIII.

IF I HARBORED ANY DOUBTS ABOUT ARTHUR'S VERACITY, THEY were swept away by what happened then. Only a god could have been responsible.

A deafening, unearthly whine filled the room, enough to drown out any argument I might have given him. The steel walls of the chamber actually began to *melt*. They were softening, dripping. Metal ran in little rivulets to the floor, collecting in small, silvery puddles—and all this was happening without the introduction of any heat! The steel was behaving like a liquid, while apparently remaining in solid form!

I stood frozen for a moment, my head splitting from the sonic assault (Dammit, I thought, why doesn't he just kill me outright?), until a drop of metal from the ceiling spattered on my shoulder. It was cold, and it crusted onto my clothing. That was when I was struck by the full extremity of my situation. The melting had fused the door shut, the intercom had been reduced to a heap of slag, and my cries for help were lost in the awful din Arthur was making. The run-off was proceeding relatively slowly at that moment, but its rate was making a steady increase. Soon the puddles would unite to cover the entire floor, and what then? Would the entire room fill, encasing me in a pool of solid steel? Would the melting ceiling cave in and crush me? Or was I awaited by a more insidious fate?

I pressed my hands to my ears. My pulse was throbbing with the horrendous noise. What was *it* for? To prevent my companions from hearing my screams for help? If Arthur thought my cries would have been loud enough for them to hear in the corridor, then he must have realized that any noise loud enough to drown them out would be *doubly* audible to those outside, and every bit as alarming. That meant he wasn't worried about what would happen if they heard me.

But maybe he *was* worried about what would happen if he could hear me himself.

It all fell into place suddenly. Arthur's circuitry included a group of semi-automatic filters which could screen out specific sights and sounds, allowing him to concentrate on other matters without any distractions. His apotheosis could have entailed a modification of that circuitry, causing it now to filter out anything which might threaten his position on the throne. Perhaps if he hadn't terminated our argument when he had, I would have been led to a conclusion which would logically negate his claim to godhood—such as a determination that God wasn't really dead. In that case, the modified filters would have sensed a threat in me, and they would have screened me out. That would explain Arthur's remark about me growing "less distinct as an entity."

The only way he could defuse the threat I presented was to kill me, and, since he couldn't perceive me, he would have to employ an indirect method to do it. That was why he hadn't just reached out and stopped my heart or done something equally direct.

But if Arthur was going to kill me, he couldn't simply let this entire chamber be filtered out of his perceptions. A part of him had to remain here, hiding in a corner or crevice, perhaps, to direct and oversee the operation. That was the purpose of the infernal noise: to shield that fragment of his awareness from anything I might say. But—*but*—if I could just find a way to communicate with that piece of his mind, he would be forced to remove it from the room entirely to escape the threat my words presented, and then the melt-off (hopefully) would stop.

Droplets were now falling from the ceiling in a light drizzle. The last patch of clear floor had disappeared. Metal was coursing down my body; I was literally *drenched* in it, funny as that may sound. I had to keep moving, or the encrusting steel would have frozen my joints in place, turning me into a living statue—soon to be a dead one. My shoes were beginning to stick to the floor, the pool of metal was deepening, and I was starting to panic. Death by slow encasement in steel was never an appealing prospect.

Then my eye fell upon the naked light bulb hanging from the ceiling. The cord from which it depended was extendable, so one could pull the light down to illuminate close work on the brain-field generator. Arthur might not be able to see or hear *me*, but if there really was a fragment of his mind lurking somewhere in this chamber, then it couldn't escape the radiant light of that bulb.

The bulb always hung within easy reach. I pulled it down, breathing a sigh of relief that the spool upon which the cord was wound had not been fouled by the melt. I crouched down in the now ankle-deep metallic soup, holding the bulb high over my head. I wanted the light to reach every corner of the chamber. Now all I needed was a simple code that Arthur couldn't fail to decipher.

I switched off the light (there was a small button on the base), then flashed it on once, for the letter A. After a brief pause, I made eighteen flashes, then twenty more, representing R and T, respectively. Next came eight for H, twenty-one for U, and another eighteen for a second R.

I had spelled out Arthur's name in a straightforward numeric-substitution code. Granted, it was a cumbersome process, but my ploy *did* work. Unfortunately, however, it didn't work as I had hoped.

Arthur recognized his name, all right—or at the very least, recognized that this was some sort of an intelligible pattern. I knew that, because the whining sound and the metallic rainstorm both intensified. Arthur knew what I was doing and was trying to stop me. The pool had reached the level of my waist as I crouched there, and I found that I couldn't straighten up, but this served only to strengthen my resolve. If I had to die, I was going to die fighting.

I went through the series of flashes again, and then again. The drippings had long since sealed my eyes shut, and I could feel the steel sea lapping at my chest. My breathing was short and ragged: metallic streamers kept clogging my nose and mouth. The only thing I could move was my thumb, and I just continued to jab it in sequence at the little button on the light bulb—on and off, on and off, on and off—

And still the metal rained down, relentlessly. It rose to my neck, to my chin, to the very brink of my lips—and then it was filling my half-open mouth. My thumb went spasmodically jerking out of control, striking the button haphazardly—

—and then I fell over, gasping, filling my lungs with sweet, clean oxygen. The noise had stopped, the metallic run-off had disappeared, and the room had reverted to normal. Arthur had withdrawn, and apparently his unnatural works could not be sustained without his actual presence.

Then I realized it was my spastic thumb that had saved me. Blind repetition of just his *name* had posed no threat to Arthur; it was only when a variation was introduced into the pattern that he had gotten scared and abandoned the chamber. Not knowing how close I was to death, he had interpreted that spasm as the beginning of a message directed at him. It was a lucky break for me.

The panel slid open, and my companions burst into the room, all wet and bedraggled from the sprinkler episode. "Cliff! What happened in here?" Mick cried. "That *noise!* Are you all right?"

"No time to explain," I breathed as he and Simon helped me to my feet. "The laboratory. I've got to get back up to the *laboratory!*"

IX.

THE INTERIOR OF THE ELEVATOR WAS COOL AND QUITE COMFORT-able physically; emotionally, however, it was anything but. I refused to tell my companions a thing, adamantly. Marie was upset, Mick hurt, Simon relentless in argument, but I would not be moved. It was the knowledge I possessed that made me a marked man; I couldn't place the same onus upon my friends. Neither could I dissuade them from accompanying me, however.

I had to take comfort in my thoughts. God was alive; I was convinced of that. Arthur's semi-conscious filters were quite obviously trying to protect him from some sort of threatening knowledge, and that argument was still the only one I could come up with which fit that specification. If God were still alive somewhere, then Arthur's claim upon the throne was void, and, being a creature of relentless logic, that knowledge would force him to step down.

But then where *was* God? He was nowhere in *this* universe, for Arthur would have known had that been the case. Therefore, after having been wounded, he must have fled into a *parallel* universe, an alternate frame of possibility—a place where he could rest, recuperate, and make plans for the recovery of his throne.

A sudden thrill of *correctness* flooded through my body. Had I not been sitting down, trying to rest briefly on the short elevator trip, I might have fallen over. As it was, I uttered a little gasp which caused the others to look at me in alarm. My entire body was tingling, *alive* with the sensation. God *lived*, proclaimed every fiber of my body, and he was working through *me*, the one who knew Arthur best, in an attempt to topple him from the throne. How else could I have escaped the melt unhurt, if it wasn't by his doing? The spasm in my thumb had not happened by chance, I now realized. It had been *God*, reaching through weakly from that other frame, doing what little he could in his wounded state to lend me aid. It would have been impossible for me to oppose the will of Arthur without his help.

But that thought directly suggested a frightening parallel: it would have been impossible for *Arthur* to oppose the will of *God* in the first place—without someone else's help.

There was a strange slurping sound from outside the elevator, and the car came juddering to a halt. The indicator panel read *3*, one floor short of where we wanted to be. "Quick!" I said, jumping to my feet. "Get out!"

But the doors wouldn't open. Mick pounded on them, and Simon punched repeatedly at the buttons, all to no avail. Then suddenly they stopped, recoiling from the walls in horror. "What's happening?" Marie cried.

The elevator was beginning to melt, that was what. "Not again," I breathed wearily. Arthur would get a zero from me for variety—but he was learning from his mistakes, I had to admit. Waiting to strike again until we were in the elevator was a clever ploy; he could remain in the shaft above us to oversee the melt, and there was no way for me to communicate to him this time.

Unless I could act fast enough—

Marie's eyes were wide with terror as the little rivulets began to flow, and Simon for once was at a loss. "Mick, give me a boost!" I directed. Forming a stirrup with his hands, the big man lifted me to the ceiling, which was just then starting to soften. I popped open the emergency exit before the melting steel had a chance to seal it shut, stuck my head through, and shouted: "Arthur! Listen! You don't know what you're doing!"

But the melt continued unabated. Damn! I thought. That meant he was hiding in the *lower* half of the shaft, *below* the car, and *still* beyond the reach of my voice. I scrambled up through the trap door and onto the roof, calling for the others to follow. Marie and Simon were boosted up, then the three of us reached down to haul up Mick.

Standing there in the shaft on the roof of the elevator car put us at the same level as the fourth-floor doors. We needed to get them open, and this was no time for logicality, artifice, cunning, or delicacy. The steel was liquefying beneath our very feet. It was Mick who rose to the occasion. There was a small glass panel to the left of the doors, a device which interfaced with the elevator controls when the car was at that level. He put his fist through it.

But even as he did so, I was thinking how easy it had been this time, quite unlike the first episode, almost as if Arthur were *letting* us get away—or herding us into his next—

The doors sprang open, and the hot blast of wind that entered flung us all against the rear wall of the shaft. Simon took a nasty crack on the skull and slumped into unconsciousness. Marie, ironically, had the wind knocked out of her, while Mick and I just got a little banged up. I helped Marie out into the corridor, having to lean full into the wind to keep my feet, and Mick slung Simon over his shoulders and followed.

No sooner had we gotten out than the roof of the elevator car, sagging beneath its own immense, liquefying weight, collapsed. Moments later, the entire affair went sliding away down the shaft, lubricated by melted metal.

The doors remained open, and the empty shaft yawned behind us like a hungry, gaping mouth, into which the hot wind was threatening to toss us. There was only one way for us to proceed—forward, directly into the heart of what lay ahead.

X.

IT WAS NOTHING MORE THAN A GAME OF CHESS, I REALIZED, with Arthur and me as the pawns. At stake was the rulership of this frame. The object was to topple the other player's king—and Arthur's manipulator, the adversary, upon whose nature I refused to speculate, was close to doing just that. God was in a very bad position here: the adversary had him on the run, and it was all he could do to stay out of check.

Now, however, we were blocked, and there was no place to run. The pawn was trapped, and with him the king. We had to find a way to break through the offense or else concede mate, and the key to this lay in determining the strategy behind the opponent's tactics. It had saved us before, but this time I hadn't a clue as to what was happening.

The entire corridor before us was filled with bubbles, little spheroids no larger than ping-pong balls. There were literally thousands of them, all different colors, some hovering, other drifting, still others winging around capriciously—but none seeming to be affected by the screaming wind that bore down on us relentlessly. They were shimmering, semitranslucent things, possessing an air, almost, of insubstantiality. And they were quite beautiful—most of them.

Nonetheless, they were blocking our path, and that made me wary. They weren't put there to be admired; there was a definite purpose behind this display, one we had to discover.

The wind, of course, was there to cover the sound of my voice, besides being an impediment to progress and a threat to life and limb. By the same reasoning, the bubbles had to be there to prevent us from getting down the corridor and into the laboratory. But how would they do it? By presenting a non-existent threat against which we wouldn't dare act?

That was doubtful. They were there to perform a specific function, and I was going to find out what it was—one way or another.

I advanced cautiously toward the first ranks of the little spheroids. I heard Mick shout something (about being careful?), but his words were torn away by the wind even as he spoke them. Up close, the things looked no more substantial than they had before; less so, even. I stretched forth my hand, wavering for a moment, then plunged it into the midst of them.

My fingers passed right through them, feeling nothing at all. It was as if the bubbles didn't even exist. I withdrew my hand, unhurt.

I looked back at my friends. "I'm going through!" I shouted, but I don't know whether or not they could hear me. I faced the bubbles squarely, screwing up my courage, and entered the fray.

Immediately, my brain was hammered by a barrage of intense and conflicting emotions, the likes of which I had never felt. Manic/depressive/euphoric/suicidal, they coursed down my nerves like fire, sending such incredibly contradictory messages to my senses that I could maintain neither orientation nor balance. I lost my footing, and the wind sent me tumbling back down the corridor.

I would have gone sailing right down the shaft had Marie not caught me, slowing my approach considerably, and Mick, with Simon still slung over his shoulders, not planted himself directly in our path. The four of us slid a few feet, coming heart-stoppingly close to the brink of the shaft, but we managed to brake ourselves in time. I clung to them gratefully as I tried to regain my bearings, my face buried deeply in Marie's wet, jet-black hair. "What happened?" she asked, lips close to my ear so I could hear her over the wind. "What was it?"

"Emotion," I said with some effort, fighting the guilty clutch of adrenaline brought on by her proximity. I spoke so Mick could hear me as well. "All different types, in conflict, given a sort of physical manifestation. It's utter chaos in there—no way to pass through without losing all sense of direction and control."

"Then we're trapped here," Mick breathed.

There was a long, nervous period of silence, broken only by the howling of the wind. "Our lives depend on passing through there, don't they," Marie said at last. It wasn't a question.

I nodded.

"I don't understand any of this," she said resignedly, and then she was pushing away from us and staggering up the corridor.

"What are you *doing*, Marie?" I cried, but she didn't hear. Mick and I could only watch mutely as she brought up before the bubbles, steeled herself, and plunged in.

She reeled for a moment, stumbled, spheroids passing through her body as if through smoke—but amazingly, she kept her balance. Slowly, painfully slowly, she straightened up, her face a mask of concentration, tilted intently toward the ceiling with eyes closed. The wind was blowing dry her damp hair, the ringlets fluttering enticingly, and her loose-fitting blouse billowed out like a sail. And then something incredible began to happen.

It was as if she had turned her body into an emotional magnet, tuned to the perfect frequency, attracting only bubbles of a certain deep shade of red. They crowded in, clustered around her like a swarm of bees—and very gradually, her body began to *absorb* them. A shimmering aura of that same crimson hue developed around her, increasing in intensity with each spheroid absorbed, until at last no red ones remained. She was a goddess, so lovely and desirable to look upon that it hurt, a hot, shining beacon blazing blood-red in the midst of a whirling storm of color.

She opened her eyes and looked directly at Mick. Her expression was rapturous. When she spoke, we could hear her voice clearly above the wind, even though it came in a husky whisper. "Come to me," she said, and the very savage sound of it sent my pulse racing, blood quickening. "I *need* you."

Then I understood her tactic: intensifying on emotion in order to subdue the rest. It *could* possibly work—but she couldn't do it alone.

Mick understood as well. "Love," he whispered, setting down Simon's body. I had to grab at it to keep it from blowing away. He moved toward Marie involuntarily, like a man in a dream. His breathing was becoming heavy and strained. "Love overcometh all."

"Yes," she exulted throatily, breaking out in a sweat. Pheromones flooded the corridor. She swallowed hard, gasping for breath. Her body trembled, writhing suggestively, and the look on her face was one of pure agonized ecstasy. "Yes, my love—*yes!*"

They surged together, and a literal explosion of passion ensued. The two of them were lost to view, a small scarlet star burning rapturously where they had stood. A voyeuristic thrill went shuddering through my body. If only that were me—

I broke off the thought abruptly, shocked at myself. This wasn't *right*—none of this was. And now I saw that certain of the less attractive spheroids were thriving in the light of the new star, while the more desirable ones were shriveling up. I was being hit by actual *physical* waves of anger, guilt, jealousy— This was *wrong*, dammit! It wasn't love going on in there at all, except by an accident of vulgar nomenclature—it was nothing more than *lust*. "No!" I screamed.

There was a blood-curdling shriek of despair, and Mick stumbled into view, backwards, fighting to keep his feet. His skin glistened with sweat, resembling a thin sheen of blood in the crimson light. His shirt was open, and his belt hung undone, libidinously. "You bitch!" he screamed in torment, falling to his knees, the wind tearing at his hair. "You lying *bitch!*"

The star was fading from view, and the bubbles crowded around it, swallowing it up, extinguishing it, forming a barrier stronger and more impassable than ever. Marie was nowhere to be seen.

Mick had his face in his hands, and empty sobs racked his body. "Ingrid!" he cried brokenly, his voice thick with tears. "I'm sorry! I *love* you—I always will. I'd *die* before this, Ingrid—I'd die for you. Forgive me." His head sank slowly to the floor.

Then I noticed the atmosphere beginning to change. Very sedate, calm blue-green spheroids were now coming to life, drifting unhurriedly over to cloak Mick's huddled form. A sensation of peace settled over the corridor, and even Arthur's hellish wind seemed to ease up a little in response.

The bubbles suffused his body with a beautiful, sea-colored aura, which slowly began to spread. Its advance was very stately and majestic, and the remaining spheroids lay helpless before it, smitten. Love overcometh all.

I picked up Simon and staggered down the corridor as fast as I could. I didn't have to examine Mick's body to know what I would find. *I'd die before this*, he had said. *I'd die for you.* It was that conviction which had saved Simon and me.

Still, I wanted to get away from there as quickly as possible, away from that aura. There'd be time enough later for grief.

XI.

THE FIRST THING I NOTICED AS THE DOOR TO MY OFFICE HISSED open was the crate in the corner. It was open. And it was empty. Van Damm was gone.

I set Simon down in one of the easy chairs, most grateful to be relieved of the weight, and crossed over to the crate. The thing was undamaged, there was no way it could have been opened from the inside, and no one had been up here to open it from the outside. So how had—?

Hold on, Peabody! I thought. Arthur had done it, no doubt.

The sound of the wind in the corridor outside was suddenly cut off as the office door slid shut. I whirled. There stood Garrett Van Damm in the flesh, looking very pleased with himself, resplendent, and quite distinguished in an immaculately tailored black-velvet tuxedo, with matching top hat and cape. It wasn't what he had been wearing earlier. "Back so soon?" he clucked. "One win tonight not good enough for you? Come to slam Van Damm when he's down, eh?" There was an evil gleam in his eye. "Well, in that case, you're in for a little surprise. I'm not such a good loser."

He produced a little black wand, gave it a flourish, and disappeared into thin air.

I took a few involuntary steps forward, glancing rapidly from side to side. "Ahem," he said, and I whirled again. He was sitting behind my desk, feet up, calmly filing his nails. "The old man is quicker than the eye." He made a little gesture with his fingers, and then his file became a smoldering cigar. He took a puff, changed it back, and resumed his filing. "Not bad for a novice, eh, Cliff? I admit it's a simple illusion, but I find it an amusing diversion."

Lord, it seemed the closer I got to the laboratory, the bolder and more audacious Arthur (or the controlling adversary) became. It was due either to increasing confidence on his part or to increasing desperation, but I couldn't be sure which. But whatever the reason, he had now chosen to pit my deadliest enemy against me, armed with what I could only describe as magic. This promised to be an interesting (if not completely spell-binding) contest.

"But when you get to be my age," Van Damm went on, "you look for diversions wherever you can find them." He chewed reflectively on his cigar. "How about *we* look for a diversion, you and I? Yes, a diversion, some nice little game to take the mundanity out of our routines. Something like a friendly game of tag—and *you*—" He pointed his cigar at me, changing it into a magic wand— "can be it."

And he vanished again.

"Now try to catch me," he said eagerly, appearing suddenly on the couch.

I didn't move; I just watched him stonily.

And then quite abruptly he was standing at the bookshelf. "Oh, come on," he urged. "Just for a few minutes. It'll be *fun*."

But I wasn't going to "play" until I knew the rules, understood what I was up against. I was dealing with an unknown quantity here. I'd wait to make *my* move until he showed a few more of his cards.

"Oh, I get it," he said, now sitting on the edge of the crate, looking like a kid whose best friend had just moved away. "You're tired of this game, aren't you? Funny, I rather thought you enjoyed it. After all, we've been playing it for the last seven years, only *I've* been it, and I've been trying to catch *you*." He sighed. "It's not much fun being it, is it." He stood up and drew a white handkerchief from his breast pocket. "Maybe I can make it a little more interesting for you."

Then he flung the handkerchief at me.

An ordinary magician would have been satisfied to produce a gentle dove from his handkerchief. Not so with Van Damm. His white cloth, in mid-flight, *became* an albino falcon—wings outstretched, talons extended, gliding straight in toward my face.

I ducked, and the bird smashed into the top of my head, its talons gouging furrows in my scalp. I straightened convulsively, grabbing for the predator—and my hands closed around the empty handkerchief. It was covered with my blood.

I swayed dizzily. That was all I had to know. Arthur seemed to be more powerful here, close to the laboratory as we were, but he still didn't dare interfere with me directly. Thus, the cloth falcon had remained animate until I took action against it, at which time Arthur had to withdraw his influence, letting it revert to its original form. He was still frightened of me, then, but that didn't make me feel any better. I was just as frightened of him.

I had a feeling that he had more magical toys for Van Damm to play with—ones I could not so readily defend myself against.

Van Damm had disappeared again, naturally. I spun full

around, but he was nowhere to be seen. "Up here," he called jauntily, waving down from above. He lay facing the floor, with his back against the ceiling. "You know, Cliff, you never were satisfied just playing a simple game of tag. *I* was doing my job, and you were always trying to damage my reputation, make me look like an incompetent—trying to *hurt* me. Well, you don't have to worry, because that's all *I* intend to do. I don't want to kill you just yet.

"I only want to *hurt* you."

I wasn't sure whether to consider that a lucky break or not.

He doffed his top hat, which was clinging somehow to his head, flattened it into a disk, and let it drop. The velvet disk fell in slow motion, rotating rapidly, developing serrations, turning shiny-metallic—becoming a spinning saw blade! The blade bobbed there before my eyes, parallel to the floor, buzzing like an angry hornet, but infinitely more dangerous. I certainly couldn't reach out and grab *this* like I had the falcon!

The blade made a couple of feints in toward my face, which I dodged light-headedly. The talon wounds in my scalp were bleeding heavily, and I was beginning to reel from weakness. The blade pressed its advantage and spun in, laying open my cheek. Hot blood spurted from the laceration, and I clapped a hand to my face in pain. Then the hellish thing sneaked in from behind to give me a nick on the buttocks.

There were spots swimming before my eyes (not to mention blood dripping into them), and my head was spinning. I could vaguely perceive the blade skimming in low across the floor for an ankle-cut or a hamstring.

I lifted my foot and stomped on the damned thing.

Van Damm's fancy velvet top hat was crushed, but I wasn't paying any attention to that. I staggered over to my desk and fell panting across it, leaving a bloody trail on the floor. The pain twisted my face, in turn aggravating the gash in my cheek.

Van Damm materialized in the center of the room, brandishing his wand like a scalpel. No, not *like* a scalpel—Lord, it *was* a scalpel.

God help me, I prayed, as earnestly as I ever had.

And my prayer was answered. As Van Damm advanced wickedly with the surgical knife, Simon was heaving himself into motion from the easy chair where I had left him. I don't know how long he had been conscious, but he was coming to my rescue now, once more. He raised his fists above his head and dealt Van Damm a two-handed blow to the base of the neck. It should have been a disabling blow, but the older man wasn't even fazed. He swung around, forgetting me for the moment, and caught Simon in a strangle hold.

It was my chance. I pulled myself to my feet, staggering across the room, and reached Van Damm just as he was slipping the scalpel between Simon's ribs. A new strength seemed to flow through my veins as I grabbed him from behind and pinioned his arms—a strength born of outrage. But even as I touched him, his magical powers were withdrawn, just as had happened with the handkerchief and the hat. The magician's tuxedo reverted to a more mundane cotton-blend suit, and the scalpel clattered to the floor, reverting amazingly enough to the heat weapon I'd taken away from him earlier. But a weapon is a weapon is a weapon.

Garrett Van Damm was in *my* power now. "You bastard!" I roared, manhandling him over to the door and slamming him up against it, his collar clenched in my fists. All the years of enmity and hatred were welling up inside me, invoking a brutality I never knew existed. "This is for Simon!" I cried, and my fist shattered the cartilage of his nose. "And this is for my wife!" One blow crushed his lips to pulp. "And this is for all the other damn things you've ruined!" My knee smashed into his groin, with all my weight behind it.

I hit the button to open the door. The wind still shrieked darkly down the corridor outside, like a channeled tornado. I held Van Damm half in and half out of the room. "Now," I said softly, "if you can think of any reason why I shouldn't kill you, just tell me, and I'll be glad to drag this out for however long you like."

Despite all this, Van Damm remained unbowed. He smiled through his broken and bloody face with all the dignity he could muster and said, as distinctly as possible: "Kill me now—it doesn't matter. But you don't know what you're doing. Mark my words, Peabody—before this night is over, you'll join me in hell."

And he laughed.

With an angry cry, I flung him out into the corridor. The wind picked him up like a dry leaf and sent him tumbling through the air, trailing maniacal laughter like smoke. I watched as his body slammed full-length into the rear wall of the elevator shaft and fell away into oblivion, four stories below.

His face left a bloody imprint on that wall—and I imagined that it was twisted into an obscene and mocking grin.

XII.

I SLUMPED INTO ONE OF THE BIG EASY CHAIRS, TRYING NOT TO look at Simon's body. I was sick at heart (and to my stomach) about what I'd just done to Van Damm, now that the bloodlust had passed. There could have been another way, I told myself. I hadn't had to kill him like that.

Both physically and emotionally, I was sinking into a sort of waking slumber, precipitated by the incredible strain I'd been through that night. My wounds still throbbed, my head, my cheeks (facial and posterior), my brain—and some of those wounds would never heal. I was steeped in blood, literally and figuratively—blood that could never be washed away. I closed my eyes and convulsions racked my body. I wanted to vomit. I felt as if I could never move again.

But I had to. I'd come here for a reason, and that reason lay in a secret chamber behind my bookshelf. People had sacrificed their very lives to get me to this spot, without even knowing why they did so. How could I not go on? Giving up now would be a slap in their faces.

I pulled myself to my feet, God only knows how, and somehow made it over to the bookshelf still upright. We'd come a long way together tonight, God and I. Behind that secret panel, I was sure, lurked something more horrible and deadly than anything I'd yet encountered—but I'd face it willingly so long as he stayed by my side.

I spoke the correct password, half-expecting nothing to happen, but the bookshelf slid aside silently, admitting me to the secret laboratory of Arthur Pendragon. The chamber was spacious and spotless, tiled in immaculate white, and it contained only four items: three large devices resembling overgrown television cameras, which I assumed were the Probability Aperture Projectors (two of them were in operation, emitting beams too bright to look upon), and one oversized leather beanbag chair.

I advanced warily into the room, and the panel whooshed shut behind me. I didn't know quite what to think. A beanbag chair, for Pete's sake! What the bloody hell was going on?

"Sit down," said Arthur kindly.

I hesitated. Maybe he was going to try to smother me in the beanbag.

"It's all right," he assured me. "I'm not going to try anything. I'm tired, you're hurt, we both need rest, and it's vital that we come to some kind of an agreement. Go on, sit down."

So I did, sinking gratefully into the leather bag, letting it mold itself around my body. For the first time in ages, I allowed myself to fully relax.

"Good," said Arthur. "I'm glad to see you treating yourself well for a change. You don't know how I worry about you, Cliff."

"That's very touching, Arthur," I said flatly, "considering what you've put me through tonight."

"Please, Cliff." That had hurt him. "You don't know what—"

"I don't *care* what! I've watched five people die tonight because of you—maybe six, I don't know."

"Six," he said sadly. "Marie was incinerated when Mick broke away from her, by the intensity of her own passion. Poetic."

"*Why?*" I cried, letting well up the grief that I'd been suppressing. "What's so *damn* important that these people had to *die?*"

"I thought I knew," he answered softly, "but I don't anymore. There was an imperative, a—a compulsion. I thought it was *right* before, but now I'm not sure. I should have been able to crush you like a *fly*, but I *couldn't*. There was something *protecting* you. You won out; you made it all the way up here, to the one place where you could make me listen to what you had to say, the one place from which I couldn't withdraw or filter you out. Leaving this room would sever my contact with the alternate frames, forcing me off the throne. You knew that, so you fought your way here, and now I'm wondering if, after all, there isn't something to what you've been trying to tell me.

"I still *think* I'm right, but I've got doubts—and those doubts are enough to make me not want to take the responsibility for whatever may happen if I'm in the wrong. There's something big at stake here, I know that much, and I'm not going to be the one to blow it—so I'm handing the decision over to you.

"But wait—I'm doing it on *my* own terms. I don't want *you* screwing it up, either.

"These are my conditions. The Department of Science has located your wife. They found her during the blackout, in a bus terminal in Reno. There was no heat, and she was near death, suffering from hypothermia. Right at this moment, the doctors are doing everything they can to save her, but they aren't going to succeed. It is within my power, however, to spare her life and restore her to you. And I will—providing you side with me.

"But if you're sure enough of your convictions, you'll stick by them, even though it means letting your wife die.

"The decision is yours."

My heart had stopped. All I could see before me was Jill's exquisitely beautiful face, floating above me, just beyond reach. It was almost as if I could touch her (like you can almost touch the stars on a clear night), stroke those silken blonde tresses, take that face in my hands— I loved her, loved her with a poignancy that defied expression. Losing her had almost killed me, and now I could win her back. There was nothing in the world more important to me than that.

But I knew in my heart that I was deceiving myself, for actually there *was* something. It was the thing I'd been fighting for all along, what my friends had given their lives for. It far transcended the life and love of one woman. To turn my back upon it would be to turn my back upon God.

My eyes were stinging as I let the lovely vision fade away, and my heart was bursting. I delivered up my verdict with a quavering voice. "I'm too sure of myself, Arthur. I have to let her die."

XIII.

"And I abide by your decision," Arthur said somberly. "What would you have me do?"

My eyes were pressed shut to hold back the tears. "Look into the gaps in your memory," I said thickly. "Bypass the filters. Find out what *really* happened to God."

It took a few moments. "My Lord," he said at last, whether in reverence or surprise I couldn't tell. His voice was soft with incredulity. "He isn't dead at all. He's disappeared into another probability."

"Because you were going to *kill* him! Because there was some other—some other *Entity* manipulating you, trying to destroy him. Now step down and let the throne be returned to God."

And, honoring our resolution—my sacrifice—he did as I wished.

Then he screamed in anguish. "Stop, you bastard!" he shrieked. "You can't do this!"

I sat bolt upright, my own grief forgotten. I'd never heard him speak like that before. I was seized by a sudden clutch of dread. "What, Arthur? What is it?"

"There *was* someone working through you, Cliff, but it wasn't *our* God! It was an evil Entity from another probability! It was deceiving you, *using* you to tumble *me* from the throne, and now it's taken over!"

The knot of dread was spreading, and I realized that it wasn't coming from inside of me, but rather emanating from the very air around me.

"I understand everything now," Arthur cried. "We were such *fools!* God saw the approach of this Entity long ago and knew that its intent was to steal his throne. Any direct attempt to repel it could have laid waste to creation, for in power they were equals, so God took measures to limit the scale of the inevitable confrontation. He maneuvered me onto the throne, so it wouldn't be left vacant, then entered another probability to draw the Entity's fire away from our frame. I became his puppet, and, in order to combat me, the Entity had to select a puppet of its own. It chose you, Cliff, and that was ultimately our undoing, for in the end your faith in it far exceeded my own faith in the correctness of my actions.

"I can't blame you for the success of its coup." His voice contained more despair than I think I have ever heard in my life. "You only did what you believed was right. The fault lies squarely with me. I wasn't strong enough in my convictions, and now our entire frame is going to suffer the consequences."

XIV.

"Listen to me!" I shouted. If what he said were true (and there was no reason in the world to doubt it), then there wasn't much time to act. The influence of the Entity was a palpable, malicious thing, every moment mounting in intensity: soon it would reach incapacitating levels. "God wouldn't have left you in charge if he hadn't thought you were capable somehow of repelling the Entity, Arthur! This is your chance to redeem yourself, but you've got to do it *now!* You represent a threat to it, and as soon as it's consolidated its power, it's going to come after you! You've got to act *now!*"

I felt a strange tugging at my hand, but there was nothing there. "You're only half right," said Arthur. His confidence was returning, and I didn't doubt for a second but that God had a part in it. "We've got to act *together,* you and I. *I* have the knowledge we'll need, that's true, but it won't do us any good at all without *your* faith to catalyze it."

There was a funny sort of a wrenching, not altogether unpleasant, and then Arthur and I stood hand in hand. Invisible lines of energy were fluctuating around us; I could almost *see* them with my body. My vision was a composite picture of many disparate images, all somehow forming one single, comprehensible whole, and sound came to me as a series of electrical impulses.

"Welcome to my world," Arthur said, and I looked at him as if for the very first time. He was young, healthy, and handsome, and the muscles stood out on his naked body like iron bands, putting me to shame. I certainly knew who was superior in *this* realm. His grip was warm and firm, radiating friendship and love. "Come along."

This was *my* creation, my legacy, my gift to mankind— And my son, for he resembled me. A lump of pride stole into my throat.

He leaped into the ether like a superman, tugging me along with him. We sailed effortlessly down electronic conduits, racing the other bits of information like little kids chasing rabbits. The suddenly we burst out into the open sky, and my vision was lost. "Arthur!" I cried. "I can't see!"

"We've just passed into the knowledge-frame," he said, giving my hand a squeeze. "Your eyes will adjust. Give it time."

And they did. We were streaking up, up, forever up, like a bipartite meteor, through an atmosphere of wisdom. The combined friction of all that information was laboring to slow us down, to divert us into the ways of knowledge, but Arthur wouldn't allow it. We streamlined ourselves, built up even more velocity, screaming breakneck, full throttle, into eternity—

And then we brought up short.

We were standing before the throne of God, and upon it sat the Entity, a being too horrible, too malicious, too *terrifying* to describe with mere words. It emanated pure evil, brandishing a serpent for a scepter and speaking with a tongue of fire. "I am beset by babes!" it cried in mock terror, and the very foundations of my soul shuddered. "Have mercy upon me!"

I cringed and would have fled but for Arthur, who stood forth boldly to proclaim: "This day will the Lord deliver thee into our hands."

Great gouts of laughter (mingled with curses against heaven so blasphemous that I am unable to record them) gushed forth from the Entity's gorge, and the wound in my hand screamed with agony. I was its puppet, its tool; I even carried its mark in my palm. *I* had killed all those people, thinking I was acting in the name of God, destroying the very people who had shaped my life, made me what I was. When (if) all this was over, how would that leave me? My hands were clapped to my ears, my face twisted with anguish. That damn laughter was going to *kill* me!

Arthur gripped my arm reassuringly, murmuring for me not to resist, to relax—and then he took me between his hands and rolled me up into a tiny ball. He applied pressure to me until all my faith was squeezed to the surface, forming a hard, protective coating. From his shoulder dangled a sling (strange I hadn't noticed it before), and it was into this that he slipped me, whipping it around his head and casting with all his might.

I hit the Entity square in the forehead, sinking deep into its skull—and then all was darkness.

XV.

I awoke in my office, stretched out on the couch. Wan, early morning sunlight filtered weakly through the shattered window, casting a fuzzy patch of yellow on the far wall. Groggily, I got to my feet and shuffled over to the window, breathing deeply of the cold, moist air. A thin, grey mist shrouded the landscape, for as far as the eye could see, defying the anemic sun to burn it away.

My world was back to normal.

I yawned, and my cheek screamed in protest. "Careful," said Arthur. "You'll pull out the stitches. I've spent a good *hour* this morning trying to get you all fixed up."

I turned around, resting my injured buttocks against the sill, regarding the room dispassionately. The bandages on my head were like a mocking crown. "We killed it, then?"

"Yes, and you should have—"

I tuned out the excited babbling that followed. Funny how someone so supreme in one realm could seem like such an idiot in another. I turned back to the window and leaned way out, heedless of the jagged glass. Arthur seemed to think we were some sort of heroes. Why then did I feel so numb? "So what happens now?"

"Now?" Arthur repeated, somewhat puzzled by the question. "Well, after the investigators have gone, it'll be business as usual, I suppose. I've had a very busy morning. I've had to alter all sorts of data files and physical evidence to make it look like we had a freak accident last night. We incurred an accidental overload, see, and *that* was what blew out the switching network—"

The cold air stung my lungs, but that was the only thing I could feel. There was emptiness all around me: sky, horizon, building, soul—

"—team of investigators arrived from the Department of—"

I couldn't stay here. It wasn't going to be business as usual; it was going to be business without Clifton Peabody. Only—I didn't know where to go. It was memory I was running from—but where do you go to escape it?

"—and all six people were killed in the ensuing explosion. What do you think of *that* story, Cliff?"

I was absently scratching the stubble on my jaw. "I think you should make it seven people dead," I said. "I don't want them to find any trace of *me*, either."

"What are you talking about?" he asked, a note of concern creeping into his voice.

I strode purposefully into the laboratory, shading my eyes, right up to PAP unit number three, the one not in use. "*Anything imaginable has to exist, right?*"

"Well, yes, but I don't—"

Why run *from* memory—when I could run *to* it? "How do you turn this damn thing on, anyway, Arthur?"